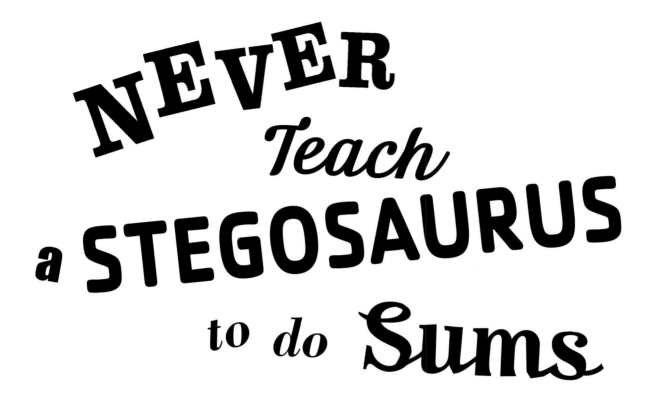

NEVER Teach a STEGOSAURUS to do Sums

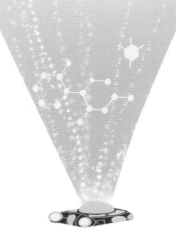

For Ishaan and Anaya, who love numbers
as much as they love words. x
R.S.

For SBE. I wish you could see this
D.E.

First American Edition 2021
Kane Miller, A Division of EDC Publishing

First published in the UK in 2021 by Puffin Books, Penguin Random House Children's.
Text copyright © Rashmi Sirdeshpande, 2021
Illustrations copyright © Diane Ewen, 2021
The moral right of the author and illustrator has been asserted
All rights reserved.

For information contact:
Kane Miller, A Division of EDC Publishing
5402 S 122nd E Ave, Tulsa, OK 74146
www.kanemiller.com
www.myubam.com

Library of Congress Control Number: 2021930472
ISBN: 978-1-68464-342-4
Printed and bound in China

MIX
Paper from
responsible sources
FSC® C018179

NEVER Teach a STEGOSAURUS to do Sums

Rashmi Sirdeshpande & Diane Ewen

Kane Miller
A DIVISION OF EDC PUBLISHING

NEVER
teach a Stegosaurus
to do sums.

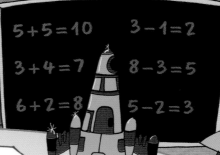

$5 + 5 = 10$ $3 - 1 = 2$

$3 + 4 = 7$ $8 - 3 = 5$

$6 + 2 = 8$ $5 - 2 = 3$

Because if you do . . .

. . . there's no end to what she might do with all those numbers.

Like **adding** them up,

STACK

taking them away,

SLICE

and a few other sneaky tricks too!

SMOOSH

And if she masters all those, she'll be having **SO** much fun that she won't want to stop!

Just you wait until she figures out how she can **USE** all those numbers and sums to crack codes . . .

bake things . . .

build things . . .

and make things
do stuff!

Who knew numbers
could do all this?

And once she figures THAT out,
what do you think she'll set her sights on next?

Ahhhh, yes . . .

She'll want to make herself a rocket
to go to the moon, Mars,
and BEYOND.

Obviously.

MOON

EARTH

WHAT TO
LOOK FOR

THE
NIGHT
SKY

Of course, she won't be able to do it alone.

SO, while she's in the mood for all that making,

and coding,

she'll build a few helpers first. Like THESE ones right here.

That's better.

Then she'll be off . . .

T-minus 5

4

3

2

1

ANNNNND . . . .

NOTHING.

OOPS.

That's OK. If at first she doesn't succeed, she'll try again.

And again . . .

AND AGAIN . . .

NEW ROCKET

Until she finally cracks it!

T-minus
5 4 3 2 1

STEG "O"
SOAR
2.0

LIFT-
OFF!

And if she makes it into space . . .

. . . she's BOUND to make some out-of-this-world friends while she's up there.

STEG "O" SOAR 2.0

She might even find they've got LOTS in common!
Because maybe . . .

just maybe . . .

A.I. ROBOT PLANS
INSTRUCTIONS
FOR EARTHLINGS

SMART
HEAD

50/50 EYESIGHT

FACIAL
SCANNING

ROBOTIC
ARM

BIONIC
LEG

$M = 0.046765 \, mol = 0.016M$

$n(B \cap C) = 22$
$n(B) = 68$

LAMBDA
CALCULUS

aliens **LOVE** numbers –
AND **ROBOTS** –
too!

and at some point she'll have to go back home.

So there will be some very teary goodbyes . . .

SNIFF
SNIFF

And if she comes back from outer space . . .

. . . she'll definitely bring some bright ideas with her!

But if she makes those robots . . .

And if **those** robots make **more** robots . . .

And **THOSE** robots make . . .

WorkerBot   ChefBot   NannyBot

EVEN MORE robots . . .

HOW TO WIRE A BRAIN

Well, **then** they'll be EVERYWHERE

BookBot

DocBot

SongBot

and things might just get
a **TEENSY** bit out of control . . .

And if THAT happens, we're really going to need Steggy to pull something out of the bag.
Because . . .

robots = fun

robots
+ robots
———————
still fun

robots
+ robots
+ robots
+ robots
———————
TOO MUCH FUN!

Hang on . . .
What's that, Steggy?

You're absolutely right!

That's why you **always** make an **OFF** button! PHEW.

OFF

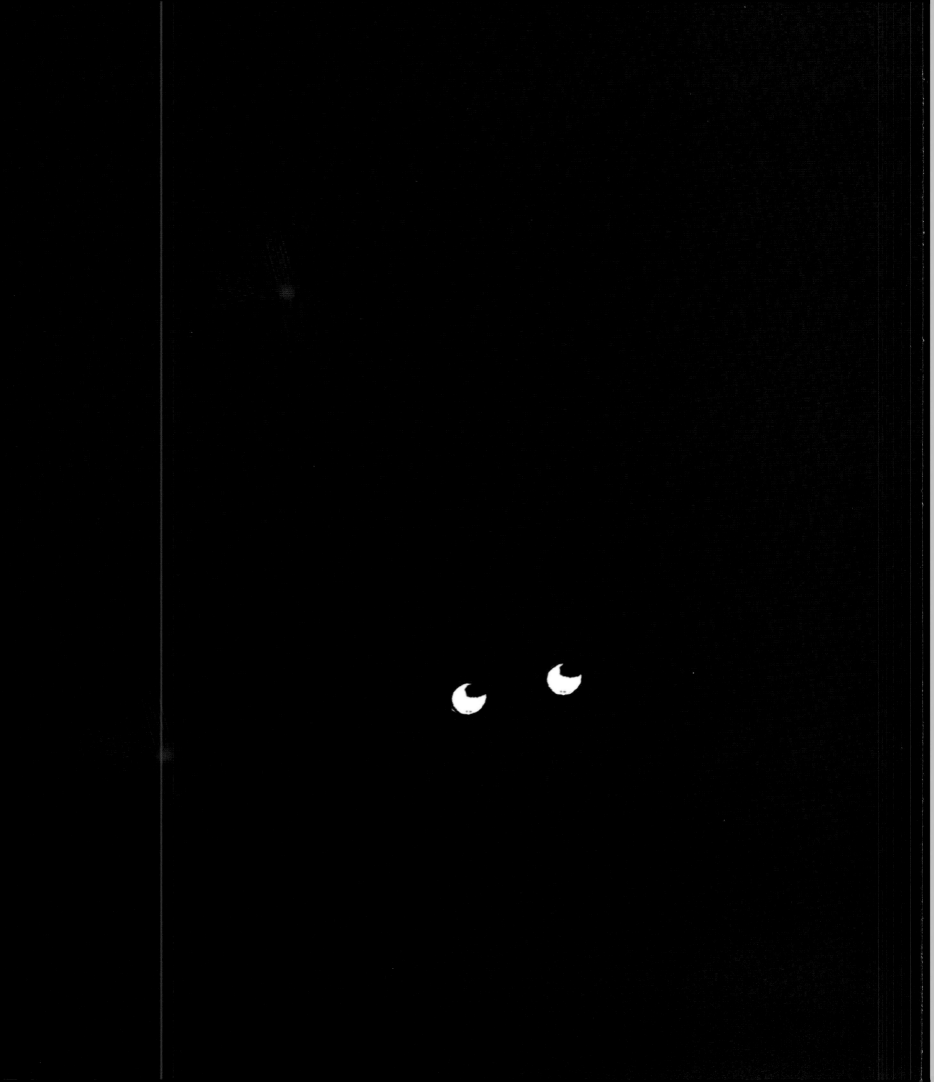

And if Steggy presses that OFF button and manages to sort out
all that mess, what do you suppose she'll want to do NEXT???

You know what?
It's been a long day, so she'll probably
want to snuggle up
and **count** the stars
in the night sky . . .

Besides, it's ALWAYS a good idea
     to save a BIT of fun for tomorrow . . .